THE HERO REBELLION 1.5

RACE

BELINDA CRAWFORD

HENDRIX & FAUST
PUBLISHERS

Published by Hendrix & Faust, Publishers in 2019

This is a work of fiction. Names, characters, businesses, places, events, locales, and incidents are either the products of the author's imagination or used in a fictitious manner. Any resemblance to actual persons, living or dead, or actual events is purely coincidental.

www.belindacrawford.com

ISBN: 978-0-6484881-0-1 (ebook)
ISBN: 978-0-6484881-6-3 (paperback)
ISBN: 978-0-6484881-3-2 (audiobook)
ISBN: 978-0-6484881-1-8 (special edition paperback)

Edited by Brendan Carney

A catalogue record for this book is available from the National Library of Australia

*For Dad, Heather
& Freckles.*

Books by Belinda Crawford

The Hero Rebellion
(Hunter)
Hero
(Race)
Riven
Regan

The Echo
Cold Between Stars
Dark Between Oceans
Echo Between Worlds
(coming 2021)

IN THE BEGINNING

Humans colonised Jørn; they travelled across the galaxy intent on a better way of life, away from the influence of Earth. But the drones they sent ahead, the ones that told them that Jørn was their new paradise, missed something; a native spore toxic to all Terran life.

Genetic engineering, blending DNA from Earth and Jørn species, saved their crops and livestock, but the colonists refused to use the same technology on themselves. Instead, they took to the skies, turning their five great colony ships into cities that floated above the spore's reach.

Times were hard. The colonists scavenged and scraped, made every morsel and every scrap go as far as it could, but it was not enough. A few brave souls risked their lives to scout the surface, locating the resources the cities needed to survive. They died in their dozens, victims of the planet's deadly wildlife and treacherous terrain.

They became known as Riders.

Now, three-hundred years later, the Riders are little more than a memory. Their legacy is kept alive in the illegal sport of street racing, a no-holds-barred test of teamwork and skill, where the only rule that matters is "don't get caught".

CHAPTER 1

Swirling strands of DNA enveloped her from head to foot. The holographic innards of the mansion's AI core were strewn about her boots, while the hot fish-scented breath of a ruc-pard snuck between jacket and helmet to stir the hair on her nape.

Hero twisted around to glare at Fink. 'Do you mind?'

The big companion twitched his rounded ears and tilted his great tawny head to the side, staring at her with the same confusion that had turned his thoughts a cloudy shade of pink. *Mind what?*

Hero huffed and turned back to the spheres of the lockdown code in her hands. 'Nothing. Just quit breathing down my neck.'

Where else was he supposed to breathe?

'Not on my neck.'

Fink grunted and moved. The gentle shift of cloud-soft fur at her back wasn't enough to jostle her focus on the tightly woven molecules spinning above her palm. She needed to tease out the chain responsible for the doors.

Hero expanded the code until—

'Fiiiink!' Her wail didn't even echo, the bio-gel in the core's datapaks absorbing the sound.

But it was crowded in here. There was a meaty thunk against the wall as he swished his tail.

She pushed off from the wall, coming up hard against Fink's chest with his head over her shoulder.

'Fine,' she said, wriggling into the deep fur around his neck. 'Just don't put your nose in the code.'

Hero took a deep breath, gathered the scattered DNA and started over.

When the first-gen colonists had mixed a bit of leopard with a bit of rat and a lot of alien to create the first 'pard, they hadn't meant for them to be stuffed into tiny closets or the even tinier confines of a modern AI's core. But Fink had shoved his muzzle in the hatch before Hero could slide it closed and now he wrapped around her like a pretzel.

His head hung over her shoulder as he watched her, the brilliantly coloured balls of DNA dancing in the deep black of a single eye.

Hero focused on the long chains of molecules coming together in her hands, the pairs linked together by thin command filaments and stacked one atop the other in an endless, twisting ladder.

She needed to find the pair that controlled the lockdown's ID sensor. A picture of the code shone in her mind's eye as she scanned the DNA, a tiny cluster of blue and green. Accessing the core had taken longer than she expected and she was running out of time.

There! The trio of blue and green spheres, wrapped in the transparent skin of their parent chromosome, leapt out at her. She plucked it out, expanding the thumb-sized parent sphere into one the size of her fist. A flick of her finger and the parent shell dissolved, leaving its guts exposed.

Fink twitched his muzzle and his whiskers cut through one of the balls in a burst of static.

She pushed his head away.

He grumbled. *He couldn't see.*

'You can barely operate a lift, what do you need to see for?'

The 'pard huffed; his thoughts turned a little sour. *He liked the colours.*

Hero did a mental eye roll. Fixated on the molecule chains that controlled the mansion's ID scanner, she opened her mind. Fink settled in behind her eyes, a sweet tangy wave of mawberry, and when she blinked, he shared her vision.

Better? She asked.

He purred, the sound vibrating through his chest before being swallowed by the datapaks.

Hero turned her attention back to the spheres, narrowing her gaze on the cluster that controlled the scanner.

Bottom lip between her teeth, she pried it out, the thin string dangling from her fingers like the wet strand of hair she had fished out of her mother's sink last week. She'd needed it and three other DNA samples to override the locks on the AI's core. It'd taken her thirty-six days to track down the right donors and another five to come up with a decoy to fool the mansion's sensors into thinking she was still in her room.

Her mother had gotten crafty recently. Tasking the mansion AI to track Hero's every move had been the start of it, but picking random DNA sequences to lock Hero out of the AI controls had been particularly devious. Most people used their own DNA, or that of a loved one, which worked well enough until someone with access to a workbench and a few brain cells decided to rob them.

The slightly smarter ones used a random food or plant, but it took real paranoia to jumble up four different DNA strands and then throw in some random junk for good measure. People that paranoid had something good to hide, or someone like Hero to keep locked in.

She held the strand of code with one hand, fighting the tug that wanted to suck the fragment of DNA back into place, and pulled a strand of her own creation out of the jumble around her wrist.

She held them next to each other for a moment. She could feel Fink still sharing her gaze, a patient, curious weight behind her eyeballs. The strands were almost identical, right down to the curious little jumble of junk DNA that the mansion AI tagged all of its subroutines with. Her mum thought it would stop Hero from doing what she was about to do.

It had almost caught her the first time.

She'd been where she was now, about to slip the replacement code into the subroutine, when she saw it. The jumble of grey spheres had woken something at the back of her skull, like a memory she couldn't place. It'd eaten up her brain and kept her awake at night until something clicked and the knowledge spilled out like it had always been there.

Hero scanned the code, taking it apart piece by piece, and smiled. The warm satisfaction of outwitting her mother lit her chest. The strands were identical, except for the little hiccup she'd embedded.

It had taken her three days to design the code to fool the ID scanner and let her bypass the mansion's lockdown. If she were lucky, it would take the AI's immune system twelve hours to find it, and if not … Hero shuddered and pushed that thought aside.

With a practiced twitch, she severed the old code and replaced it with the new strand.

The core flickered. Hero held her breath, Fink holding it with her. The air pent up in their lungs as the new strand zipped into place, the molecules closing up around it.

For several tense heartbeats the DNA didn't move, didn't flicker, just turned an ugly shade of puke grey as the AI's immune system swept through it.

Five heartbeats.

Six.

Nine.

Hero counted them out in her head. The air started to burn in her lungs, trapped there by the tension riding her skin. Getting caught fooling around with the mansion's AI wouldn't be as bad as blowing up a chunk of the city, but this time there wouldn't be any sympathy from her mum.

Thirteen.

The sick weight of dread began to curl in her stomach. Had she missed something? Had her mother changed the tag, or maybe there was a step she'd skipped, a security measure she hadn't noticed?

The air was fire in her chest and she had to take a breath, but tension was gripping her throat and the dread had wrapped sticky tendrils around her lungs.

Hero's vision turned black at the edges. If this didn't work …

Colour flooded the core, rising through the DNA in a wave of pink and blue and every shade in between.

The breath left Hero's lungs in a gusty rush to rival the tornado that left Fink's.

She sucked in another lungful of air and let it out as her heart settled back into place, before twisting around and giving Fink's wide, tawny chest a push. His chest was bigger than it had been eight months ago, the fur deeper and coarser. She did her best to ignore the puckered scar that marked where the bullet had entered his chest, and pushed back against the memory of Fink on the ground, blood staining his fur as the kidnappers dragged her away.

Fink purred, disrupting the memory and replacing it with another of Hero curled up with him in front of a holo-fire. The remembered feel of his fur under her cheek and the soft rise and fall of his breathing chased the other memory back into the recesses of her skull.

She rested her forehead against his neck before straightening. 'Come on,' she said. 'There's not much time.'

Fink grunted and shifted enough for Hero to scramble over his backside, only narrowly avoiding tripping over his tail as she reached the room's control pad.

She hesitated before opening the door.

Hero lowered her mental shields and with Fink still sharing her mind, let her thoughts seep through into the mansion beyond.

Fink's mind moved with hers, his mawberry-flavoured thoughts shadowing her, guiding and correcting her technique with gentle nips at her telepathic heels.

Together they mentally moved through the mansion, sliding through her mum's office to the bedrooms before heading down the curving staircases. Sweeping through the five-hover garage, the kitchen, the bedroom and jerry-rigged lab that made up Hero's domain, they checked for the telltale pops of light that signalled waking minds.

All was silent, even Chef wasn't in the kitchen, nor was Tybalt in his suite, doing something serious and no doubt designed to curb Hero's fun.

Hero popped open the door and out she and Fink rushed, snapping back into their own heads as they did so.

They were in her mum's office, with its cherry-red chairs and shelves full of smelly, Old Terra books. Hero didn't waste time stopping to admire the view of the gardens, or to luxuriate in the shaggy carpet under her feet. She grabbed the backpack stashed under a chair and picked up the helmet wedged between it and the bookcase.

Her helmet squawked as soon as she put it on, as a comm came through.

'Hero?' Norah's voice hissed in her eardrums. 'Where are you?'

Hero opened the channel and a vid of her best friend popped up on her visor. 'I'm—'

'You're *late*.' Norah was speaking low, head ducked and shoulders hunched, as if there was someone else listening in. 'We're already here. Hurry.' The line went dead.

Adrenaline shot through Hero's veins. She had her backpack on in almost the same second it took her to leap onto Fink's back.

'Run,' she said.

As ill-suited as 'pards were to squeezing into small closets, they were even less suited to racing through small doorways and down tight spiral staircases. Hero held on for grim life, even when her knee banged into the doorjamb and sent darts of pain all the way to her toes. Fink stumbled on the last step of the staircase, almost throwing Hero over his head. Only his mid-paws saved them from skidding across the foyer on their noses.

There would be claw marks in the soft, red-veined marblewood, she was sure of it, but Hero didn't have time to worry about that now. If she were lucky, the cleaning bots would buff them out before her mother got home, and if they didn't ... She'd worry about that when she got back.

Fink bounded across the massive atrium where all her mother's staid, powerful friends exclaimed over the floating chandeliers. At the other end, a small red 'lockdown' holo was visible against the giant plasglas doors that led to a pristine acre of lawn.

She had to time this right ...

Five metres to go.

... far enough to give the doors time to open ...

Four metres.

... and close enough that they wouldn't snap shut on Fink's tail.

Three.

They'd have a split second, all the time she'd been able to trick the ID scanner into thinking she was her mum, before they triggered the alarm.

Two.

'Abracadabra,' she yelled.

The doors opened.

One.

They were through, the edge of the sliding plasglas grazing her knees as they passed. Fink landed heavily on the immaculate lawn, leaving divots in his wake. Hero hoped the garden bots were as vigilant as the house ones.

Bounding past the flowerbeds, they wound their way through thick blue-green shrubs towering taller than her and Fink combined. They skidded to a stop in front of the giant grey wall that encircled the property.

Hero jumped off Fink and ran her hand over the steelcrete, searching for the hollow that hid the control pad. She found it.

A chunk of the wall slid into itself, revealing another world.

The noise hit Hero first, the rumble of the waiting taxi and the rush and blare of hovers beyond, before the lights assaulted her eyes.

Even during the day, with the sky a bright blue above, Cumulus City created its own blaze, but at night it truly was a dashing multitude of colours to stun the senses.

The side of the taxi split open. Norah hung out of the boxy hover with its massive 'T' holo overhead. 'Hero!' she yelled, jolting Hero out of her daze.

Hero dashed across the small half-circle of steelcrete that served as the mansion's tradesman's entrance, scrambling into the taxi with Fink a half-bound behind. His tail was barely in the hover when Norah slammed the hatch closed.

They lifted off, the taxi's engines taking on a higher pitch as the vehicle rose from the hover pad and then descended into the city.

CHAPTER 2

Norah fidgeted on the passenger bench, tugging at the high collar of her jacket. She sat across from Hero, her back to the bulkhead that separated them from their driver. There was sweat on her forehead, a worried tilt to the straight black line of her brows and a jittery tension to the spill of her thoughts that made Hero's skin crawl.

'Would you stop that?' Hero snapped.

Norah jerked her attention away from the dark, sparkling view out the small window and frowned at Hero. 'We almost missed the first clue because you were late. If we miss the second, we won't *find* the race and if we can't find the race—'

'We'll get there.'

'Maybe.' Norah chewed her thumbnail and jiggled on the seat. 'We need to place in the top three to qualify for prelims and if we don't get to them ...' Norah let the sentence trail off.

If they didn't get to the prelims they had no hope of qualifying for the biggest street race of the year, the Twilight Cup.

Hero shifted in her own seat, the thought of the Cup sending nerves and excitement through her veins in equal measure.

The Twilight Cup was the pinnacle of street racing, but that wasn't what excited Hero. What excited her were the scouts that were rumoured to stake out the Cup, on the lookout for new talent to fill the ranks of the Pro Racing Circuit. The Pro Circuit was a hop, skip and a leap from Hero's goal to explore Jørn's surface. Just her and Fink, with no one to tell them what to do or where to go.

Freedom.

But before they could win the race, they had to find it, and quickly before the markers that led them there faded into nothing.

The clues had started off as a security measure, a way to stop the police from breaking up the races. It had since become as much a part of the street races as the parties and the racers themselves.

A loud ping echoed in the cab. Norah slapped her bracer like someone had bitten her. The other girl's visor flipped down in the same second, light and motion playing across the inside.

Hero leaned closer, crawling over Fink to get a better look.

Before she could make out more than Rom's long, thin face, the image cut out.

Norah punched the taxi's intercom. 'Umm, hi? We're going to Mina Plaza instead.'

A screen flickered to life in the middle of the cab, fizzing where it cut through Fink's rump. Instead of a human face, the smooth emotionless features of an AI stared out at them. Hero's heart jolted in her chest before she realised it wasn't the Librarian on the screen but the taxi's AI.

'The driver is currently unavailable.'

'No, I'm not,' Said a sleep-fogged voice. The face of a woman old enough to be Hero's great-grandmother replaced the smooth, digital features of the AI. Her tanned face was wrinkled and saggy, at odds with the smooth dome of her head.

The driver rubbed sleep out of her eyes. Hero guessed she'd been asleep until a minute ago, leaving the taxi's AI to do the driving. 'It'll cost you, and Mina don't let none of them big ones in the plaza,' the driver said with a lift of her chin towards Fink. 'Not after them street racers banged it up last month.'

At the mention of street racers, the old woman cast a long, meaningful look at the helmet on Hero's head. Hero leaned back and crossed her arms, resisting the urge to glare by reaching out and touching the driver's mind. Fink reached out with her, a gentle guiding presence as she shifted through the old woman's surface thoughts.

The woman was thinking that the kids in the back of her cab looked a little young, and a little too posh to be street racers, what with the fancy bracer on one of them and even fancier boots on the other. But still … there was that helmet, all sleek transparent plasform like the pro racers used, and the 'pard. The 'pard made the woman nervous and doubly grateful for the thick plasteel bulkhead between her and her passengers.

There weren't many reasons for a kid to have a 'pard, what with all those claws and teeth and their ability to sneak into a person's head.

Hero's gaze narrowed, like she could burn a hole through that bulkhead. She sensed the woman make a decision to call the police. Hero's hands turned to fists. No longer content to listen, she arrowed through the driver's skull, straight for the decision to call the police, and grabbed tight.

Harish bit her nose.

'Ouch!' She moved to slap the flyer away, but he was already airborne and her concentration was broken.

Fink rumbled, his head resting on the other seat as he looked at her out of one reproachful black eye. *They did not force their will on others.*

Norah glanced from Fink to Hero, lifting a hand to stroke Harish as the 'adder slithered into his favourite spot around the girl's neck. 'What was all that about?'

'Nothing,' Hero said.

Manners, Fink said at the same time.

'Okay.' Norah glanced between the two, confusion evident on her brows. *What really happened?*

Hero wrinkled her nose at the lingering menthol flavour in Norah's otherwise lavender-scented thoughts and wondered when her friend was going to ditch the meds. *The driver knows we're street racers. She's turning us in to the police and Fink didn't let me stop her.*

Norah's fingers stilled in Harish's crest and her face lost a little of its normal golden glow. Hero wasn't sure if it was the mention of police, or the thought of how Hero might have stopped the woman that made alarm spike through Norah's brain.

Resentment flared in Hero's chest at the possibility of it being the latter. It'd been six months since their kidnapping, six months since Hero had *saved* them from their captors. Norah still acted like Hero was some kind of monster whenever *that* incident came up, as if she was going to turn around and suck the brains out of the next person she saw.

Hero crossed her arms and turned to look out of the thin slice of window.

It wasn't like she hadn't felt bad about it, or as if the memory of blood trickling out of the man's nose and the way he'd dropped to the ground, boneless as a rag doll, didn't haunt her sleep. Even now the sound of his mind *popping*, the flood of his memories and the way they'd been sucked into the dark crevice at the back of her skull scared her. Scared her almost as much as the first time she'd done it.

Hero hugged her chest tighter.

Norah didn't know about that. Fink didn't either and she intended to keep it that way. She didn't need more of Norah's fear. She didn't want to know how her best friend would look at her if she ever found out about the green-haired woman.

'Mina Plaza coming right up girls.' The driver's voice echoed through the cab, making Hero jump. 'Looks crowded. We'll have to wait a few for a landing pad to open up.'

Hero craned her neck to peer out of the tiny, slot-like windows in the cab's side to get a better view of the landing pads. She couldn't see much, just a slice of the massive skytower that housed Mina Plaza, its shiny steelglas sides covered by shifting holo-boards, each one flirting with the crowded skylanes. But no matter how she twisted and angled her head, she couldn't see the landing pads until Norah reached around her and pressed a yellow spot on the door. It flickered and the bulkhead was gone and they were staring out at the chaos and bluster of Cumulus City's core. The endless thrust of the skytowers packed tight around them and the skylanes were jammed with traffic.

'Thought you knew everything,' Norah teased.

'It's a taxi,' Hero said. The ancient vehicle was barely worth her time. She scanned the crowd around the semi-circle of taxi pads. *There*, she said to Norah. She didn't point but threw the image of the blue mini-hover she'd spotted at her friend.

And there's an open hover pad over there. Norah sent a mental image from the other side of the taxi.

Hero studied the police mini-hover making its way through the crowds, her visor picking out the handful of security bots bobbing along in its wake. *The driver's stalling, giving the police enough time to get in place so we can't escape.*

What do we do? Norah said.

I don't know. Hero glared at Fink. *What do we do Mr Smarty 'Pard?*

Fink yawned. A memory of Hero in the AI core, twisting balls of light spinning around her hands, appeared in her brain as the taxi landed.

She could do that to the taxi, he said.

Hero glared harder. *It would've been easier to stop the driver.*

Fink snarled at the same time that Norah punched Hero in the arm. She jerked away from them both, rubbing her biceps. 'Ow!'

Norah returned her glare while Fink flipped his tail in agitation. Even Harish poked his head through the dark fall of Norah's hair to give her a hiss.

'Fine.' Hero gave her arm one last rub. 'But I'm pinning it all on you if we get caught.'

'Get caught at what?' The driver's voice boomed in the cab, and Hero turned her stare to where the holo-cam should be.

A smile stretched across her mouth and without even stretching her mind, she sensed the old woman start at the menace in the gleam of her teeth.

Hero's bracer sprang to life.

There wasn't time for finesse, and it was too late to worry about covering their tracks. The old woman had been asleep when the taxi had picked them up but the taxi's AI had a record of their faces and knew where she and Norah lived. Not even the ID scrambler in Hero's helmet could fix that.

The taxi was starting to move towards the hover pads and in the corner of her eye, Hero could see the police getting closer and closer.

Turn your gear off. All of it. Hero sent the thought to Norah.

Her friend didn't hesitate and as Norah's visor and bracer went dark, Hero pulled a small egg-shaped drone from one of the pockets across her chest. It was easy to hide from the holo-cam but not so easy to hide the display above her bracer. The hover pad was right under them now, the downdraft from the taxi's engines sending little flurries of air across the platform and causing the security bots coming up the ramp to bob and shake.

Fink rose to a half-crouch, muscles tensing, while Norah all but vibrated on the chair beside her.

Hero shut her own bracer and helmet down with a flick of her thumb.

'Alright girls.' The driver's voice crackled with tension. 'Now, don't do anything stupid, you hear?'

The first police officer reached the ramp.

'I'm doing you a favour here,' the driver continued. 'Street racing is gonna ruin your lives.'

The side of the taxi split open.

Hero released the drone.

Too quick to see, it shot out of the cab before the door was fully open and hovered above the landing platform, a shiny black egg quivering three metres in the air. For several long seconds, everything stopped.

One.

Two.

Three.

BOOOM!

Hero was out of the taxi before her bones finished rattling, Fink was a split-second ahead of her and Norah a split-second behind. The police's mini-hover stuttered and died. Behind them the taxi hit the landing pad with a resounding thud, its lights dark, its circuits as fried as the security bots smoking on the ground.

Hero smiled but didn't stop to gloat. The police were already untangling themselves from their mini-hover and Norah was swinging a leg over Fink's back, the 'pard half-crouching to make it easier for them to get on. Hero scampered up in front of her friend and they were off, Harish winging his way ahead.

People and bots scattered as Fink bounded through the shoppers, the police yelling at them to halt. The mall loomed ahead, holoboards bright and colourful against the dark.

A holographic lagoon stood between them and the mall's giant maw, full of fake Old Terra palms and sparkling water, with benches for shoppers to sit on. Harish dived through a palm tree, green and orange wings sending shivers of static through its giant fronds. Fink plunged in after him. Hero was unable to stop her reflexive flinch as he charged through the tree's ridged trunk.

Water spewed up at Fink's feet, drenching Hero's boots. Not the whole lagoon was a holo then. Hero looked down and her breath caught at the sight beneath them. The bottom of the lagoon was transparent steelglas and through it she saw the bright lights and darting shapes of a busy skyline. For a second, it was as if they were galloping on air.

Then Fink was thundering out the other side of the lagoon, up the wide, crescent-shaped steps and through the mall's neon archway.

Up and up the mall rose, bridges and walkways extending into a darkness that rivalled the skylane they'd just galloped over. Holos and drones zipped above, blending into a never-ending, restless movement of people silhouetted against the flash and pop of advertising.

Parents, kids and companions eddied around them while bots

laden with bags trailed behind boys, and clusters of girls giggled on escalators. Tall, short, skinny, fat, they all scattered before Fink like leaves before a breeze, scrambling out of his way with snarls and curses.

Hero ignored them. Her gaze was on the map spread across her visor, her attention split between the path appearing there and Norah's whispers in her ear.

'The map's revealing itself as we go,' Norah said. 'Keep going straight until I tell you. Harish will scout ahead for trouble.'

Hero nodded, leaning a little lower over Fink's neck and merging her mind into his. Just like in the AI core, they shared senses, but instead of Fink sitting behind Hero's eyes, she now sat behind his, trusting Norah to guide them.

They sprinted into the throng, Fink bouncing this way and that, dodging people, carts and companions like they were shock sticks at full charge. Norah held tight to Hero's waist.

'There!' Norah thrust her arm over Hero's shoulder. An image of a wedge of darkness running between two of the mall's giant wings appeared in Hero's mind.

The saddle harness cut into Hero's thighs and a frantic 'Eep!' escaped Norah's lips as Fink cut sideways, leaving Harish to double back towards them.

Windows sparkled on either side of the wedge, reflecting bright golden lights that made the shadows deeper, taller and thinner, until Hero wondered if it was even a corridor at all or simply a shadow.

Four strides away from the wedge and she was sitting up, ready to pull Fink back.

Three and she had her hand fisted in his ruff, an unspoken 'Stop!' trembling on the tip of her mind.

Two and the wind of Harish's passing buffeted her cheeks.

One and the linch-adder passed into the darkness.

Then they were in, the sides of the narrow corridor almost brushing their knees. Her visor adjusted to the lack of light and there, at the end, was Harish clinging to a hover drone.

Norah released her death grip on Hero. She glanced back to see Norah with her bottom lip caught between her teeth, eyes on the wall ahead as she fiddled with her bracer. Behind her, black against the purple and white flash of the police hover, came the unmistakable figures of people running towards them.

Hero swung her gaze forward to the rapidly approaching wall. 'I don't know what you're doing,' she said. 'But hurry up.'

'One. More. Second.'

The drone Harish perched on flashed green and the wall slid into itself.

They escaped into the service corridor beyond.

CHAPTER 3

An old service lift whisked them downwards. Large enough to hold half her mum's fleet of hovers, the big boxy crate was little more than a steelcrete frame and as cold as it was noisy. Hero huddled into Fink's warmth, frozen fingers tucked under her arms, wishing she'd been able to get her hands on a nanoskin–the kind that stuck to the wearer's flesh like Old Terran tar and would keep them toasty even if they were frozen inside an ice-block. She might have been able to fleece one from Bayard if it hadn't been for the incident with the mini-hover she had 'borrowed'.

She didn't know what had gone wrong. Rewiring the mini-hover to make it go faster should have been easy. She could see the new circuits in her head, laid out like an old, blue memory as if she'd done it a thousand times. Her fingers had taken over from her brain and then she must have blacked out because she couldn't remember how she'd mixed up the hover's power circuits with the maglev generator. All she knew was that when she turned the hover on, it exploded.

Hero shivered and stamped her feet. The expression on her mum's face when she'd seen the crater in the garage floor wasn't something she wanted to think about. That was around the time her mum had grounded Hero and put the mansion on lockdown for good measure.

'How much longer?' Hero yelled, over the clatter of the service elevator.

The wind whipped Norah's breath away before it could frost in the air. 'We're almost—'

The lift shuddered and slammed to a halt, throwing them to the ground.

'—there,' Norah finished, from where she lay sprawled on the bottom of the lift.

Hero groaned and peeled herself off the floor.

The lift doors, twice as wide as they were tall, shifted back with a rusty, shuddering screech. Light spilled in through the slowly widening gap, a glaring kaleidoscope of colour. The roar of a crowd and the deep, chest-jarring thump of music replaced the bone-rattling thrum of the lift.

In the opening, a boy-shaped silhouette loomed over them.

'You're late.' The boy's voice boomed out of his too-skinny chest. 'Run into trouble?'

Hero recognised the voice and the dull gleam of the bio-comp wrapped around the boy's throat. She squinted against the light, her visor darkening as she scurried to her feet and pulled Norah up with her.

Rom's thin face and shaved head came into view.

'Police,' Norah said, dusting her hand on her pants before thrusting her palm out for Rom to inspect. Their street racing credentials spun over her glove, a holo of a 'pard and 'adder. 'Our taxi called them on us.'

'Huh.' Rom waved his long fingers through the holos, his eyes focused on the data that began scrolling across his visor. 'Cops have been sticky ever since last month's race, so I've brought in extra eyes.' He gestured over his shoulder and Hero lifted her gaze to stare at the small, head-sized drone over his head.

It was shiny and smooth but instead of reflecting the wildly coruscating lights, the drone absorbed them, reflecting its surroundings like some kind of camouflage. If Rom hadn't pointed out the drone, Hero doubted she would have seen it.

'Race starts in fifteen minutes,' Rom said. The holo above Norah's palm glowed pale green. 'You'll get the course map in fourteen. Better saddle up over here or you won't make it through the crowd.' He cast his gaze back over his shoulder. 'Things are going to get rowdy tonight.'

Norah and Hero rode Fink through the mass of people who'd come to see riders, scouts and companions race through the bowels of Cumulus City. Hundreds of spectators were jam-packed in the tiny spaces between skytowers, while floating holoscreens showed the competitors milling at the start line.

The scent of sweat and alcohol permeated the air, burying the smell of dust, roaches and the garbage that piled high against alley walls.

People parted around Fink, pressing up against walls and sucking in their stomachs to let him pass. Wide eyes and comments followed them, the kind that would have been whispered if the grinding music hadn't forced them to yell.

No one trusted a Woolsey. They feared them, watched them with awe and counted every heartbeat until they passed, but they never trusted them.

Hero wondered what the onlookers would do if they knew not one but three of the first-gen scientist's genetic creations were brushing past their shoulders.

The door at the back of Hero's brain cracked open, and a hard thread of blue slipped out from where she'd shoved the green-haired woman's memories, when she had *popped* the woman's mind all those months ago. For a second, she saw the crowd as the woman might have seen them, and felt something dark and scary stir within and feed on the crowd's imagined fear.

A punch on her arm brought Hero back to herself.

'Hey, wake up,' Norah said as she slipped off Fink. 'This is it.'

They stood in an alley not quite wide enough for the fifteen assembled race teams. Racers and their companions squeezed between the skytowers, riders and scouts huddled together over screens that they kept away from prying eyes, while the companions talked to each other. Amongst the sleek sterdanes, spindly doe-ocs and oad-hawks with big eyes and wide lips, it was the sinuous purple tail of the toa-mare, Phara, that caught Hero's attention.

The 'mare stood tall and proud, a cross between an Old Terra equine and something large and scaly, holding herself aloof from the other companions and clearing the surrounding space with long, lazy sweeps of her tail.

'Looks like Dane is here,' Hero said.

Norah didn't look up from arranging the holoscreens above her wrist. 'We knew he would be,' she said. 'You did pack *all* the kit, didn't you?'

Hero patted the pouch strapped to her thigh. She wore an identical one on her other leg and, in pockets across her chest, there were two more drones of the type she'd unleashed on the taxi. Their weight was a comforting presence that summoned blue memories from the dark recesses of her brain.

A yell rose from the crowd behind them. Separated from the racers by a wide holographic strip, the spectators danced and eddied. A few scrambled for places up against the tape, seeking the best view of the start line, but most were content to jostle for the space above the racers' heads.

Between skytowers, what should have been pitch-black space, punctuated only by the occasional glimmer of an old service bot, was a shifting riot of stars. Drones in all shapes and sizes fought for space.

The drones would be a constant during the race, streaming the action to their controller's screens and to the bigger ones over the crowd's head.

Something shimmered amongst the drones, dozens of little head-sized somethings slipping in and out of the crowded airspace. Hero narrowed her gaze and she thought she caught a glimpse of one of Rom's drones.

Harish's screech brought Hero's attention back down to the

starting zone. The 'adder was dive-bombing an oad-hawk, a stumpy-looking flyer with a wide-lipped mouth and glossy brown feathers. Its webbed feet looked set to strangle the arm of the boy as he tried to shelter it with his body.

Phara reared over the boy, the toa-mare's short blunt teeth snapping at Harish's tail feathers. Her hooves clattered on the ground and her long tail cleared the space around her in angry sweeps.

There was another shriek as Harish turned his attention from the oad-hawk to dive at the 'mare's eyes. Fink was already moving, pushing other racers out of his way as Norah yelled at Harish to stop. They'd gone several paces before a long jet of water pounded Harish in the chest, tumbling the 'adder out of the air. Norah caught him before he hit the ground, a hissing, spitting mess of wet feathers and lashing tail.

For a moment, everything was silent. Even the blare of the music seemed to dim; Hero imagined the cloud of drones overhead slowly switching their focus from the wet tangle of Norah and Harish to the boy with the water gun in his hand.

Tall and lean, Timon Dane's black hair was only slightly darker than his skin and a few shades lighter than his scowl.

'Hey dude, keep your 'adder under control.'

'Your oad-hawk started it,' Norah shot back.

'He was just playing,' Timon said.

'You were sabotaging us,' Norah shot back. 'Or do you have another reason your scout was aiming *this* at Fink?' Norah held up a yellow disc the size of her thumbnail.

Behind her, Hero sensed the crowd suck in its collective breath on a wave of anticipation. It buzzed down her spine and fizzed in her gut, filling her with a dark, heady glee before a mawberry nudge reminded her to close her mental shields.

'That's a lie!' Timon Dane's scout, Henry, the boy with the oad-hawk, drew himself up, still clutching the 'hawk to his chest.

'I have it on vid,' Norah said.

Argument broke out as Henry got in Norah's face and Timon tried to slide between them while the other racers stood back and watched. Anticipation surged up Hero's spine on the multi-coloured breath of the minds that made up the crowd. It filled her head to bursting, making her skin seem too small and calling to the hard thread of blue at the back of her psyche.

Hero squeezed her eyes shut, blocking it out as best she could. She strengthened her shields again, filling the holes in her concentration and reinforcing the separation between her mind and the crowd.

The hard blue thread receded. When Hero opened her eyes, it was to focus on the little disc in Norah's hand.

Hero nudged Fink forward until they were at Norah's shoulder. The argument stopped, words dying in the scout's throat as his eyes fixed on Fink. Fink extended his nose, gently whuffing in the boy's face until he shrank back, retreating behind Dane and the bulk of his toa-mare.

Fink whuffed again, extending his nose further only to jerk it back as the 'mare snapped at him.

Hero ignored them, leaning down to pluck the disc from Norah's fingers. It sent a tingle over her skin. She held it up to her visor, but even before the code started filling her screen, she knew what it was, knew it like she'd known about the junk DNA in the mansion's AI. An inexplicable knowledge rose from the back of her brain; another memory that wasn't her own.

Hero had a vivid mental image of the disc sticking in Fink's fur, making him convulse as it scrambled his nervous system.

Trepidation slithered through Hero's gut while her heart raced with anticipation. The emotions clashed in her chest, pushing bile up her throat and making her hands shake. Concern rolled off Fink, the sweet mawberry of it pushing back the nausea.

'Racers.' Rom's voice boomed in her helmet. 'Take your places.'

Hero slipped the device into the back of her glove.

'Fans.' This time Rom's voice echoed in the crowded alleys. 'Are you ready?'

A roar greeted him, swallowing the thumping music and bouncing off the skytowers. The sound of it rippled down Hero's spine and spiked her blood with adrenaline. Her heart beat faster and nervous excitement danced in her stomach. Norah shot her a smile filled with the same emotion and threw Harish into the air.

A yellow and white holotype marked the start line. Hero joined the fifteen other racers. A honey-coloured sterdane growled with excitement on her left, while a spideruck puffed out and fluttered its feathers to her right, its eight many-jointed legs quivering in anticipation.

Nerves ran in the air, carried in sharp, high-pitched voices and the shuffle and stomp of companions. It settled in the back of Hero's mind, a fizzy, multi-coloured cloud that she could taste. It all merged with the nerves in her stomach, adding weight to the roiling ball already there.

Norah popped up on the left side of her visor, looking serious but excited, while another screen appeared on the right, streaming vid from the cam on Harish's harness.

'We have the map,' Norah said. 'Get ready.'

Hero nodded, pushing aside the nerves in her stomach to focus on the course ahead. Beyond the start line was another long, thin alley, its shadows punctuated by dim, yellow lights. *Not long now*, she thought to Fink.

He rumbled back, excitement and tension rippling through his fur.

'Racers.' Rom's voice echoed in her helmet and a split-second later, through the alley.

The outlines of three spheres appeared front and centre of her field of vision as the last ripples of sound faded. 'Are *you* ready?'

Yells and raised fists burst out of the surrounding riders, with roars from the sterdanes and a piercing hiss-nee from Dane's toamare. Above Harish shrieked a war cry, but neither Hero nor Fink made a sound.

She crept into the back of his head, a light touch that let her sense the rough surface of the alley beneath his paws and see the dark arcade stretching ahead.

'The race starts in … Three.' The first sphere turned a solid red. 'Two.' On the second count, the crowd counted with him. 'One!'

Fink launched forwards, his giant muscles bunching and releasing to propel them into the pitch darkness.

Fur and feathers moved with them, the spideruck and the sterdane jammed in at their sides. Fink leapt ahead, the massive muscles in his rump pushing them into the lead by a neck and then a body-length, leaving the sterdane snapping at his tail.

The view on her visor shifted, no longer showing the dark arcade in front but the racers behind, calculating distance and optimum trajectories.

A little more, Hero thought.

Fink grunted and pushed himself harder. The distance widened.

Out the corner of her eye, Hero caught the sleek purple of Dane's 'mare. The pair were pulling even with Fink as the fierce acceleration offered by a 'pard's greater muscle mass gave way to the speed of companions bred for racing.

It was now or never.

Hero reached into the pouch attached to her leg, fingers closing over three little spheres. 'Now,' she said.

On her screen, Norah nodded.

On Harish's screen, Hero watched the dizzying feed as the 'adder dived at Fink's rump.

Hero threw two of the spheres into the air.

At the last second Harish turned his dive into a swoop, catching the little coloured balls in his talons and looping back. Hero twisted in the saddle and threw the last sphere with all her might.

The spideruck and sterdane lurched in opposite directions, but not fast enough. The bomb exploded in mid-air, a sharp burst of light that lit up the alley in stark shades of black and white. It would have blinded Hero, like it blinded the racers behind her, if her visor hadn't been set to polarise at the right moment. She watched the sterdane stumble into a doe-oc and the spideruck run into a wall.

Other racers who hadn't caught the full brunt of the blast fared better. Some leaned over their companion's necks, urging them faster, while others reached for the pouches strapped to their own legs and two scouts aimed their flyers at Hero.

None of them saw Harish swooping out of the darkness or the little spheres in his talons.

The bombs dropped amongst the pack like assassins, unseen until it was too late. One exploded in a puff of violet fury that enveloped the doe-oc, the other in a violent green blaze that spread under the other sterdane's paws like an oil slick. Both went down in a tangle of legs, tails and riders.

Hero turned her gaze forward. Across the other side of the alley, Timon Dane had pulled ahead, a 'pard-length between them and the distance was growing. The rest of the field–those still standing–began to pull even with Fink.

'Three down,' Norah said. 'Eleven to go.'

Hero frowned. 'I saw four.'

Norah shook her head. 'The spideruck recovered.'

'We should have aimed for Dane,' Hero said, eyes on the distance opening up between them and the boy's toa-mare.

'His scout's too good, and that 'mare of his is fast. We'll have to catch them at the shortcuts.'

'Can't Dane's scout see them too?'

'Probably, but Rom's encrypted them. If I can crack it before he does, we're set.'

'Use the Rabbit.'

'What?'

'One of the programs I loaded onto your bracer.'

'When?'

'Last month.'

'Last month? How—Duck!' Norah yelled, a half-second before Hero's visor flashed a warning.

Hero ducked and felt the rush of air as a sphere the size of her fist passed her cheek.

Fink leapt sideways as the spider-bomb hit the ground and white goo burst under his paws.

She was pulling another sphere out of her pouch before Fink touched back down, throwing it upwards for Harish to scoop out of the air.

Hero watched him on her visor as he looped backwards, using the spectator drones above as cover, ducking and weaving through the flyers that tried to stop him,.

Light flooded the arcade before Harish reached his target. Through the comms she heard his screech, even as Fink stumbled, falling to his knees with the light stabbing into his night-adjusted eyes.

The light was too bright, pulsing in a pattern that brought bile to her throat and made her head pound. Her visor tried to compensate, but the polarisation only cut the glare and did nothing for the disorientating strobe.

Hero looked up. There were hundreds of drones overhead. The spectator bots were dark blobs while Rom's drones pulsed with the force of the sun. He'd made them part of the race, a trap to navigate.

'What do we do?' Hero asked Norah.

'Hang on, Harish has found—Harish!' Norah yelled in Hero's ear. 'He's down. I think he flew into a wall.'

'We'll get him,' Hero said. Fink tried to stand but his forelegs wobbled and his knees hit the steelcrete once more. She needed to take out Rom's drones.

Something rammed into them from behind.

The impact threw Hero forward, the straps over her legs barely keeping her in the saddle. Fink yowled, the sound high and pain-ridden. Through their shared link, Hero felt the fire burn up his spine and the sharp crunch of something breaking under the weight of a hoof on his tail.

The weight vanished a heartbeat later, but the pain continued to sing all the way up to his ears.

Anger gripped her chest.

The hard blue thread at the back of her head surged forwards, overtaking her vision and—

Hero blinked.

The strobes were gone, the alley with them. She was launching Harish skywards, turning in the saddle to see the alley in the distance, dust and debris choking the air.

Fink galloped over a skybridge, pain still dogging his thoughts. On her visor, Norah was thunderous.

'—you do?'

'What?'

'What. Did. You. Do?'

'I don't—'

'Penalty.' Rom's voice boomed inside Hero's helmet. 'Team Hero, three-minute time penalty for dangerous tech.'

'What? But I didn't do anything.'

'You took out half a wall.' Norah glared at her.

'I—'

She had. Fink shot her a memory. There she was, pulling one of the black, egg-shaped drones from a pocket across her chest and bringing the holoscreen to life above her bracer.

She couldn't see what was on the screen; the strobes interfered and Fink's angle was wrong. But he'd caught the almost malicious gleam in her eyes and the alien blue-colour of her thoughts as she programmed the drone.

Then the memory changed and she was scooping up Harish and leaping back into the saddle, the little black device hovering over their heads, doing something to the light so it didn't pierce his eyes.

Another cut in the memory and Fink was galloping out of the alley, the skybridge a haven of soft light ahead of him.

He watched the drone fly back towards the alley, where it exploded. He felt the boom in his paws before rubble and dust spewed out of the alley to choke the air.

The memory ended.

Hero blinked. *But … why don't I remember?*

'Hero!' A hint of worry had dislodged the anger creasing Norah's brows. 'What's wrong with you? Wake up!'

'Wha—'

'Turn right. Now!'

They were almost over the skybridge, and ahead was another long, dark arcade. To their right was a slice of darkness cut into the side of the skytower and the bioluminescent glow of Timon Dane's toa-mare racing away into the black.

Fink was already turning, all six paws scrambling for purchase as he skidded around the corner.

Light burst above them. Hero threw her arm up to shield her eyes even as Fink flinched and started to slow. She waited for the nauseating strobe but it didn't come. The blaze dimmed to a gentle glow. It was a large sphere attached to one of Rom's drones. She scanned it, but no warnings flashed on her visor.

'This is the shortcut?' Hero asked as Fink picked up speed, racing after Dane.

'Yes. That Rabbit thing you installed cracked it.' Norah frowned. 'Here.' A map replaced Norah's image on the visor. A yellow line twisted away from the main course, ending in a blinking red dot and a mess of static.

'Where's the rest of the map?' Hero said.

'I think we have to reach the dot first.'

'A checkpoint?'

'Yeah.'

'Dane's going to get there first.'

'Not if we can help it,' Norah said, her image replacing the map. 'You kept that device they tried to stick on Fink, didn't you?'

'I did.' Hero pulled the little disc from the back of her glove. 'Harish will have to get close, and he's not going to have much time.'

'How much exactly?'

'Sixty seconds.'

'We'll do it, just get ready.' Norah was silent for several seconds, communicating with Harish off-screen.

On the other screen, Harish chirped and swooped towards Hero. 'Slip-skin first,' Norah said. 'We'll come back for the disc.'

Hero fumbled a green sphere out of the pouch on her leg and threw it for Harish. He snatched it out of the air and was gone, wings pumping as he sped after Dane.

Fink followed Harish down the dark alley, his breath coming in sharp pants and his hearts pounding away between Hero's knees. Above, Rom's drone with its big, white sphere kept pace.

Green light blazed around Timon. Phara let out a high-pitched squeal and then the light sank into the floor, forming an oily green blanket across the alley.

The toa-mare skidded across the slip-skin, scrambling for purchase even as her hind legs slipped out from under her.

Hero winced as 'mare and rider went down hard. She focused on Harish's yellow belly as he dived at her head, banking hard at the last moment with his talons outstretched.

She tossed the little disc in the air, ducking as Harish grabbed it and looped back to deliver the next blow.

Dane's oad-hawk dived at Harish, the two becoming a tangle of feathers and tails as Fink reached the slip-skin.

The disc fell from Harish's talons, Hero's visor tracking it as Fink leapt.

It missed Dane, sending up an arc of electricity as it landed on the slip-skin instead. Her visor noted the surge of power that coursed through the skin, spitting out a warning as the field grew. And then they were sailing over Dane.

A jolt of alarm went all the way to Hero's stomach as she saw the determined grin on his face and the spider-bomb in his hand.

There was just time for Hero to suck in a breath and another moment for Norah to yell a warning before white goo exploded in her face.

It splattered across her visor and got in her mouth, tasting like marshmallows and wet 'pard. There was no time to spit it out. She experienced Fink's alarm as the white strands bound to his legs, saw the floor rushing at them and the slip-skin extending into the distance. She sensed Fink's desperate twist and the sharp bloom of pain as he met the steelcrete with his shoulder.

Hero was thrown free, the straps holding her in the saddle releasing before Fink hit the ground.

More pain, this time riding up Hero's neck as she landed hard. Instead of rolling to a stop, the slip-skin ensured she kept on skidding as the dark skylane whizzed past. The sick green of the extended slip-skin lit up the corners of her vision. Rom's drone kept pace overhead, dangling its big white sphere.

The sphere changed colour, a single sharp green pulse.

'Hang on,' Norah yelled. 'The sphere's the checkpoint! Harish's going to get it.'

Hero grunted, yanking at the web that held her and Fink together. 'I'm. Not. Going. Anywhere.'

The spider-bomb held Hero and Fink together for a moment, the strands stretching as she spun away from Fink. Half a metre became a full metre, as gravity pulled them apart.

Phara barrelled through the space between them, snapping the web.

Part of it cracked back into Hero, sending her into a spin. Overhead, she saw Harish knock the sphere from the drone before Norah flooded her vision.

'You're at the checkpoint,' Norah yelled. 'The rest of the map—' Norah's face drained of colour. 'Oh crap,' she said.

The floor fell away.

CHAPTER 4

They plunged down the slide in a tangle of legs and tails, neither 'pard nor 'mare able to gain purchase on the slip-skin.

For a moment, she was caught between Phara's tail and Fink's forepaws, spinning around and around as first one then the other gained traction and quickly lost it again. And then, with a huge push, Fink threw her back up the slope, free of the tangle of 'pard and 'mare, though not as far as the rectangle of light they'd fallen through.

Hero fell after the companions, her hands grabbing uselessly at the slick green energy field that had followed them in. She saw the silhouette of Timon above and caught the flash of two dark shapes above him. She twisted onto her back as one flew overhead.

The slip field highlighted Harish's underbelly in shades of green, glinting off the two white spheres clutched in his talons.

'Brace yourself,' Norah said in Hero's ear.

'Wh—' A weight slammed into Hero's back, knocking the breath from her lungs and turning her into a spinning top. She recognised the burnt orange of Timon's mind even as she felt his arms wrap around her and attach a device to her chest.

'Hit it!' Timon yelled and then he let go.

He spun away and Hero caught sight of a similar device attached to his own chest before he slammed his palm to it.

Light exploded around Timon and he shot into the air, enveloped in a thin skin of white. Hero's visor picked up the distinctive energy of an anti-grav field before he passed through the now tiny rectangle of light and disappeared.

Below her, two more explosions lit up the endless dark. She saw Fink rocket upwards in his own bubble of anti-gravity with Harish wrapped around his neck. Hero didn't waste another second, smashing her palm against the device on her chest.

The anti-grav bubble ripped her upwards, the air rushing past her ears in a roar of sound, the force of it pressing her flat against the bottom of the bubble like one of Chef's pancakes. She burned out of the darkness into the dim light of the alley, but still the bubble didn't slow. It sped up, heading straight for the pitch black of a freight shaft. This time, the anti-grav bubbles above leavened the darkness, their brilliant white glow highlighting massive steelcrete columns and the thinner lines of power conduits.

She could see Fink, Phara and Timon above, all racing up and up and up.

'Norah!' Hero yelled over the rush of air. 'What's going on?'

There was no answer. The comm was full of static. Data streamed down her visor almost too fast to see, but she caught the jagged wavelength in the bubble's DNA that was scrambling the comms. Lips pressed tight, Hero reached for her bracer, fighting against the press of air holding her down. She was still jacking into the bubble's code when they left the freight shaft behind.

Darkness gave way to the roar of hovers as the bubble burst into a skylane. Glaring lights and the blare of horns blinded Hero. She blinked her eyes clear in time to see a barge bearing down on her, its broad white nose filling her vision.

She curled in on herself, but the impact never came. The barge swerved. Hero twisted about as the bubble continued upwards. The vehicle veered into oncoming traffic, creating a snarl of hovers. More chaos spread in her wake like the tail of a human-sized comet, the blaring horns and knotted traffic showing her trail of destruction.

So intent was she on the mess below, Hero didn't see the solid shaft of energy forming at the top of the bubble. She noticed the skin of the bubble underneath her thinning, the pressure lessening against her back and twisted around in time to see the glistening bottom of a pond rushing at her face.

She burst through the steelglas in a shower of shards and water, the bubble dissolving around her. There was a moment when she was flying on her own, before gravity took hold and she was plummeting straight towards the jagged hole in the pond and the skylane beneath.

Out of nowhere, a purple blob smacked into Hero's ribs and yanked her sideways, halting her plunge into the abyss.

Whether it was the impact of the grab-lasso or being slammed into the tiles surrounding the pond, the force squeezed the air from Hero's chest. She lay on the steelcrete, panic clawing inside her chest as she struggled to breathe. Her lungs were stuck together with nanoglue and she thought she would never experience the rush of oxygen again.

Timon appeared above her, his black brows drawn and his forehead wrinkled with concern.

Determination obliterated panic as air rushed back into Hero's lungs. She fumbled with the pouch attached to her leg, fingers seeking the short, fat object stashed there.

Timon crouched by her side and even as she took in her second wheezy breath, she brought the stunner up and—

The boy dodged to the side, the stunner only grazing his arm.

Hero rolled to her feet, stumbling as the world swam around her. Her vision turned grey and then white, before colour seeped back in. She took one lungful of air and then another after that, her vision clearing with every breath. She looked around.

They were in some kind of plaza. The busted pond sat at its centre and four of its six sides were fronted with white-tiled shops. The other two sides opened out into alleyways, the distant hubbub of a crowd echoing off their walls. In the plaza, half a dozen people were staring at Hero and the chaos around her, some had palm-units out, taking vids, while others rushed to where Timon lay sprawled on the ground.

No-one approached Hero as she stood, water dripping off her, the stunner clutched in her hand. She was grateful for her helmet's ID scrambler as whispers of 'police' echoed in the silence, gaining volume as they passed from lip to lip.

The crowd's curiosity reached out to her, pressed against her skull in mental waves. She strengthened her shields but still they pressed—

At the sound of hooves, Hero spun towards the alley behind her and gripped the stunner tighter. Fink burst of the archway, his coat wet and Phara hot on his tail.

The people taking holos scattered as he barrelled through them. Those attending Timon tried to protect the boy with their bodies, but Timon was already rising to his feet as Hero half-ran, half-stumbled past him.

Fink slid to a stop and Hero threw herself into the saddle, even as she watched Timon reach for his 'mare.

Harish screeched overhead, the bright sphere of a Violet Night clutched in his talons. Fink was already racing back the way he'd come before Harish delivered the bomb. It exploded in a puff of purple fog, missing Timon and Phara but catching the crowd who'd gathered around. The 'adder looped back, talons outstretched and an imperious warble emanating from his beak.

'Throw him the other Violet Night,' Norah said, popping back up on Hero's visor.

Hero dug the last one out of her pouch and threw it high.

Harish snatched it out of the air, but instead of doubling back to hit Timon, he flew onwards.

'Where's he going?' Hero said. 'And where've you been?'

'Trying to get around the comm freeze,' Norah replied. 'And as for Harish …' Her lips tightened. 'I had to drop the comm encryption, the line isn't secure. You'll have to wait and see.'

Wait and see. Hero didn't like those words, they made her

stomach churn and her fingers itch to reach for her last remaining drone and see for herself. But Phara was clattering up Fink's tail and Dane's oad-hawk was diving at her head.

Hero ducked and swung the stunner, felt it hit the flyer's tail. She hoped she'd made contact long enough to deliver the shock.

Then her helmet flashed a warning and popped a new screen, showing her the 'hawk as he dived again, another spider-bomb clutched in his webbed feet. Hero swore and jerked Fink to the side, straight into Phara.

The 'mare squealed. The stunner fell from Hero's grip and the spider-bomb went off where Fink had been a second ago. White sticky threads caught on Hero's boots and splashed over her leg. Through their connection, she felt others stick in Fink's fur and under a paw, making every stride a little harder as the threads tried to glue him to the ground.

Hero's helmet flashed again and she turned in time to block Timon's throw.

A third spider-bomb gleamed between his fingers.

Hero yanked his arm down and Fink moved with her, sitting on his haunches. They skidded to a stop as Phara galloped on, yanking Dane out of his saddle.

Hero felt the boy's surprise, the moment of confusion as he became airborne. The brief glimpse he had of his 'mare's rump, the thwack of her tail as he toppled backwards, then the brief second of realisation that he was falling and that it was going to hurt.

Hero let go before he hit the steelcrete. Part of her winced in sympathy, while the other, darker part grinned in satisfaction.

Trouble. Fink's thought was as breathless as he was, carrying with it the heavy pounding of his twin hearts and the burn of exertion in his muscles.

She didn't have to ask him what the trouble was. The thick musk of a dober-shepherd flowed from Fink's nose to hers. The scent got stronger and stronger, overriding the sweet, salty smell of humans.

Dober-shepherds meant only one thing.

Police.

Fink burst out of the alley into another plaza, a nano-copy of the first, complete with storefronts and shoppers, except for the police-woman sprawled in a dissipating puff of purple fog.

The dober-shepherd skirted the edge of the Violet Night, whining and snapping at the fog as he tried to get to his rider, but careful not to touch it with more than his paws.

The companion turned as Fink rushed out of the alley. His whine became a growl, the thick hair around his neck standing on end.

This plaza was smaller than the one before. The immobilised policewoman and her growling dober-shepherd blocked their way through the middle, while shoppers crowded the edges. With no clear path through, Hero narrowed her gaze and urged Fink forward.

He went straight through, leaping over the unconscious woman as her dober-shepherd charged them from the side. The 'shepherd's jaws snapped millimetres from Hero's boot. She kicked him in the snout. The companion yelped.

Fink thundered around the corner and burst into Mina Plaza.

CHAPTER 5

The crowds, holo-cams and drones were thicker than before, filling the endless arcade with noise and light. They were crammed together in a chaotic eddy of people and tech, shifting first one way and then the other, forcing Hero to hold on tight as Fink leapt and jerked in a frenetic dance, trying to force his way through the crowd.

Her head hurt from the noise, the lights and the press of thoughts. Hero tried to strengthen her shields again, digging deep in her core until only the soft mawberry of Fink's concern shared her brain.

I'm fine, she said. Except for the exhaustion pulling at her bones and the pressure forming at the base of her skull, but she kept that to herself.

Overhead, advertisements shouted wares and promised sanctuary from the crushing throng. Harish zipped through them, disappearing amongst the holos.

Norah hovered on the inside of Hero's visor, concentration drawing her brows together and tightening the set of her mouth. The rest of Hero's visor was clear — no map, no yellow or red triangles marking out traps in the chaos — revealing only an endless sea of people that made tension crawl up her spine.

'Well?' she finally asked.

'You're still on the course.' Norah bit her lip. 'I think.'

'You think?' The tension in Hero's nape twisted and she couldn't help but look over her shoulder. 'We're in Mina Plaza, Norah. There are cams and police everywhere!'

'It's the shortcut. This part of the map is still encrypted.'

'Use the Rabbit.'

'I already did. We need a key or a checkpoint or something, but it's not giving me any clues!'

'Send it to me, then.'

'I don't think that's a good idea. The Rabbit picked up something weird in the encryption.'

The purple and white of a police hover flashed in the distance, filling Hero's voice with urgency. 'Just send it!'

'Fine.' Norah gave in and the information flooded Hero's visor.

For a handful of heartbeats, the race map spread before Hero, showing their path in a crazy string of dots. She focused on the shortcut, her mind already whirling with possibilities as she activated her bracer.

Strings of DNA rushed past her eyes, twisting and turning on each other. There was no time to swear and barely enough to recognise the virus before it overtook her helmet.

More and more strings joined the first, replicating themselves over and over until they swamped Hero's vision with chromosomes and molecules, blotting out Fink and the plaza. And then the sound started, a high-pitched whine that rang in her ears.

It came in waves, pulsing in time with her heartbeat and each was louder than the last until it screamed in her head, vibrating her bones and making her eyes cross.

Hero ripped the helmet from her head, strings of DNA still twisting in front of her, the vision seemingly burned on her eyeballs, while the screaming echoed in her ears.

She didn't see the drone until it hit her in the stomach.

Air blasted out of Hero's lungs and she snapped backwards onto Fink's rump, with only the harness stopping her from being thrown off. She clutched the kamikaze drone in one arm and her helmet in the other as, for the second time that night, she found herself winded and looking up at the holo-studded darkness.

A sweet mawberry nudge, rich with concern, came from Fink and then he was slowing, the rush of people in her side vision slowing with him, the press of the saddle in her back easing. It was just enough for Hero to draw the breath back into her chest, before she caught the distinct purple and white strobe of the police hover closing on them.

Go, Hero said, the thought packed with the same urgency that dried the spit in her mouth.

Fink went. His first bound included an extra bit of bounce that threw Hero upwards. She used the momentum to right herself, doubly thankful for the harness across her thighs as she strained against the straps, the tension pulling her upright.

She flopped forward, ignoring the pain in her back. The drone buzzed in her grip, trying to free itself, but Hero held on tight, glancing at it long enough to identify that it was one of Rom's. She hooked her helmet onto a belt loop and took in the scene around her.

In the few seconds she'd been prone, the crowd had been parted by a parade of police drones and a mini-hover with two officers screaming right down the centre.

The crowd formed a human canyon, its walls a seething mass of curiosity and holo-cams. Fink spun on his haunches and charged the sides.

Shoppers tried to scatter but ended up tripping over their bags or running into their neighbours. Fink leapt over them. They were airborne for a heartbeat, long enough for Hero to meet one man's eyes, to sense his panic pounding at her brain. Then Fink was bounding through the mall.

People screamed and yelled, *their* panic coursing towards her mind along the same path that the man's had. Some snuck through before Hero could shake them off.

Fink leaped sideways, jerking Hero back to the mall as he glided over a short bench to crash through a holographic tree behind it, before racing back into the crowd.

Hero sought Harish's bright yellow tail amongst the drones and holos. Where was he? Her helmet was still a riot of colour, the whine still tickling her ears. With no comms, Harish was her only link to Norah.

Do you see him? She sent to Fink.

His answer wasn't a word so much as a breathless collection of images that all amounted to one thing. *No.*

Hero swore again. Without Norah or a map, they were a sitting spideruck waiting for the police to catch them. The door at the back of her mind popped open and a thought slithered out. *Unless …* Her arm tightened around Rom's drone.

But she'd need time.

She stood in the saddle, trusting to Fink to warn her of oncoming drones and cast her gaze about.

There. The holographic palm grove blazed in her mind's eye. She nudged Fink towards it even as she reached into her pockets for the last of the little black drones.

Hero kept one eye on the mall as people and their companions leapt out of Fink's way. Drones bobbed and darted overhead, and the purple and white police hovers closed in on them. The rest of her attention she devoted to the drone in her palm and the screen above her wrist.

She needed something stronger than an electromagnetic burst this time, something big enough to distract the crowd *and* the police. The whisper at the back of her mind agreed, and Hero found her fingers flying over the holoscreen, twisting the drone's DNA without thought, following the plan seeping out the door at the back of her psyche. It was alien and yet somehow a part of her, as if she'd done this a hundred times before.

As the drone flew from her hand, Hero shared her plan with Fink. He skidded to a stop just metres from the grove, refusal in his thoughts.

A moment was all he had.

The drone exploded, sending a shockwave through the mall.

Lights flickered, people screamed and Hero leapt off Fink, using the chaos to drive into the grove.

Fink stood rooted to the spot.

Find Harish! Hero yelled at him, adding a push for extra measure.

He snarled as the push bounced off his shields, but leapt back into the chaos anyway. He was lost to sight before Hero had a chance to turn away.

She settled deeper into the grove, making herself as inconspicuous as possible amongst the dense holographic grass and palm trees.

The holograms splintered and fuzzed where she knelt, but if she didn't move she would be invisible.

Invisible like one of Rom's bots.

The drone continued to buzz and shake in her grip and she wondered if Rom was looking at her now, if he had her face plastered across those massive holoscreens above the crowd as she tore his tech apart.

The access port was easy to find, embedded in the top of the drone's casing. It opened with a gentle push, sliding aside to reveal the bright yellow pulse of the tech's brain and the dull, pale indent of an input.

Hero dug a thin thread of bio-gel out of her pocket, using it to connect the drone to her bracer.

Like that, she was in. No firewall, no immune system, just a command prompt appearing on the screen above her wrist.

'Your programming sucks,' she told the drone and hopefully Rom beyond. Or maybe Rom had left his tech defenceless on purpose, because slipping into the drone's DNA like that was too easy. But she'd take easy right now, because the next part … the next part was hard.

Hero teased out the code that controlled the drone's camouflage. If she could extend it, create a bubble big enough to fit herself and Fink inside, they could get out of this mess with ease.

If only she could concentrate.

Hero rubbed her forehead, trying to ignore the multi-coloured buzz of the people around her. There seemed to be more now. The weight against her psyche grew heavier as outrage mingled with a new sense of alarm and a sound like a dozen hoof beats. The colours and flavours of their minds streamed past, each one different, distracting her from the task at hand.

With her attention split, she blacked out for a moment. In the dozen heartbeats between opening up the chromosome controlling the drone's camouflage and collapsing it again, a thick blue haze that reminded her of the green-haired woman coated her mind's thoughts. She knew she was changing the code and that the camouflage bubble would cover their escape, but she wasn't aware of *how*.

There was no time to ponder that though, even if she'd wanted to. The colours and flavours of the crowd were sneaking through her shields. She tried to strengthen them, tried to layer another line of defence under the thick sheet of psychic energy already there. It worked for a moment, and she was free to focus on the drone in front of her before the pressure came back. More minds joined the others and Hero realised, as she sensed the new wave of non-human minds, that the race was coming through the plaza.

Laser-focused and running on adrenaline, they stampeded towards her. Not just flavours and colours this time, but images and impressions of riding a sterdane, ducking the paper-thin wings of a flurry-thyt, her nose going numb as a Violet Night exploded at her spideruck's feet.

They squeezed her skull under their collective weight, a vise against which the pressure strained. It was a ball of energy at the base of her skull, clogging up her brainstem and slowing the commands from her brain to her hands, making her fingers clumsy. She fumbled the code and the camouflage activated before she was ready, but instead of forming a shimmering bubble around her, the drone began to pulse with light. Every flash of light, dim at first but gaining strength, made her head hurt anew.

The drone wasn't supposed to do that. It wasn't supposed to *pulse.*

The pressure on her mind grew with every flash of light, seeping from the back of her head across her cheekbones to grip her eye sockets, climb her temples and *squeeze.* It squeezed so hard she thought her eyeballs might pop out.

A whimper slipped out of her throat and Hero gripped her head as if she could grab hold of the vise gripping her skill and tear it away.

There was so much noise, so many minds swarming around her. She was drowning in a kaleidoscope of colour, new flavours assaulting her nose with the relentless pound of the racers' companions. If only she could shut them out, close her mind like she closed her eyes, but no matter how she reinforced her shields, the noise hammered its way through.

Hero clapped her hands over her ears. The pressure strained at her skull, making her scalp too tight and her hair hurt. She needed to hold it together, just a little longer … just until Fink got back.

Hero saw the drone flash. It was as bright as the sun, illuminating the inside of her closed eyelids and assaulting her senses.

Hero lost the battle.

The blast ripped out of her skull. All the noise and all the colours stopped.

Hero slumped over her knees, relief and exhaustion flooding her veins in equal measure. The pressure had vanished with the noise. It left her limp as a noodle and she sat like that for a second and then two, before the silence began to crawl up her spine.

Hero lifted her head. She could hear people yelling for help in the distance but her eyes were stuck on the chaos beyond her hiding spot.

Bodies littered the mall, slumped and sprawled over chairs, the floor and each other. Companions had collapsed mid-stride, some riders thrown clear of their steeds, other slumped over necks or saddles, all unmoving except for the smooth in and out of their chests. Hero didn't know how far it went, but she could see people beyond, running and yelling for help.

Had she done that? But how? She remembered the drone flashing. Had she programmed it so poorly? Maybe she'd made some kind of mistake in the seconds she couldn't quite remember and turned the camouflage bubble into a flashbang, the burst of light stunning anyone who saw it. Or had it been something else, like the mental blast?

The clatter of hooves broke Hero out of her trance.

Phara cantered through the mall, slowing as Timon sat up straight in the saddle, bringing the 'mare to a trot and then a jerky walk as they approached the swath of unconscious bodies. Even at this distance, through the obscuring sway of grass, Hero could see the shock on his face, the questions, and for a moment it seemed like he had found her amongst the holos.

He pulled Phara to a halt, and it looked like he was going to jump off.

Then the piercing wail of an emergency drone broke the silence and with a look over his shoulder, Timon urged his 'mare back into a canter.

Tension drained from Hero's shoulders, but only for the time it took the emergency drone to come to a stop right over the grove.

Hero swore. The emergency drone meant more than police, it meant ambulances and the news crews that would inevitability follow. But what spurred her was the distant wave of mawberry-flavoured urgency coming her way.

Whatever happened, she couldn't let Fink see what she'd done, or Norah—

Hero's heart squeezed, a painful constriction that seemed to take her breath away and replace her blood with adrenaline.

There was no time for anything fancy. With Rom's drone clutched in both hands, Hero rose and threw the drone upwards with all her might.

It smashed into the emergency bot.

She winced at the crunch of plasform as the drones collided, but didn't stop to gauge the extent of the damage. Running, leaping over bodies, eyes fixed on a slither of shadow between two shop fronts, Hero only hoped the collision was enough of a distraction to cover her escape.

She made it to the narrow service access without someone yelling at her to halt. Heart pounding, breath coming in pants, she pressed her back to the wall and tried to melt into the shadows.

Fink was out there somewhere; she could sense him coming closer.

'Hero!' The tiny squeak came from around her knees and Hero remembered the helmet hanging from her belt. Strands of code still played across its surface, turning the transparent platform into a psychedelic riot, but the high-pitched whine had stopped, replaced by the frantic sound of Norah's voice.

'Hero!' Norah's yell almost had Hero yanking the helmet back off. 'What are you doing? Why did you go offline?'

'I—' Hero stopped, wet her lips and replied. 'The map was rigged. It gave my helmet a cold.'

'I *told* you it wasn't a good idea.'

'You did,' she said. 'Just get me out of here!'

'Give me a second. There's some kind of barricade up ahead ...' Norah's voice trailed off, leaving Hero with the riot of code still taking over her helmet.

The swirling lines of code were giving her a headache. She deactivated the visor, the plasform splitting down the middle and sliding into the rest of the helmet.

The first stirrings of exhaustion were winding through her bones but tension still kept them at bay.

'Okay.' Norah's voice in her ear sent a burst of adrenaline through her veins. 'I'm sending you a map, it's—'

'I can't see it,' Hero said. 'My helmet's still infected.'

'Oh.' Silence played through the comms. 'Right, well, stay there until Harish finds you.'

Movement above the crowd drew Hero's attention. A drone flew through the air, the faint shimmer disturbing the air underneath it. Her heart thumped before trying to crawl up her throat. Hero didn't need her visor to recognise the telltale signs of a scan in progress.

Hero backed down the alley, hoping she could lose herself in the darkness. 'The police are scanning the crowd. I need to go now.'

'Alright. Listen to me very carefully.' Norah said.

Hero stepped out in the crowd with Norah whispering directions in her ear. She kept to the edges, doing her best to lose herself in the constant eddy of people, keeping her head down and resisting the urge to look over her shoulder. No one took much notice of her, everyone too busy converging on the spectacle of street racers passed out in the middle of the mall. That didn't stop the tension massing at the base of her neck or the itch between her shoulder blades that hinted at someone watching.

Just keep walking, she told herself. Fink wasn't far, the mental scent of mawberries was getting stronger with every stride. No one was looking at her, no one was looking *for* her—

'Hey, you! Stop!'

Hero ran, pushing, ducking and weaving her way through the crowd. Norah was still in her ear, but Hero had stopped paying attention. Fink was somewhere ahead of her, and the dance of his thoughts across hers was all the direction she needed.

Boots pounded behind her, a drone flew overhead.

Hero pushed through a couple too busy peering at their palm units to see her coming. And there, beyond another scattering of people, was Fink.

A drone dropped into her path, a stunner protruding from its nose. Hero skidded to a halt, arms windmilling. A screech from above and the flash of Harish's tail grabbed her attention just as Norah yelled, 'Duck!'

Hero dropped to the ground.

Light exploded. The flash left stars in her eyes, but against it she caught the silhouette of a man reaching out to grab her.

Then Fink was there. Stars still obscured her vision, but she felt the soft brush of fur and the touch of mawberries. He crouched so she could leap into the saddle and then they were off.

CHAPTER 6

The flash bomb that Harish had dropped gave them time to evade the police and escape into the relative safety of Mina Plaza's service corridors. It felt like an age of winding back and forth through the maze of dark, narrow passages before Norah got them past the cordon now encircling where Hero had … exploded.

None of them relaxed for a moment, and by the time they stumbled into another freight elevator, leaving Mina Plaza behind, Hero trembled with tension.

After that, the rest of the course was almost anticlimactic. A swarm of wasp-bots descended on them as soon as they got off the freight elevator. But while evading them made her heart pound harder it didn't come close to the sight of all those bodies lying in Mina Plaza.

Fink sprinted for the soft rectangle of light at the end of the alleyway, snarling as the bots stung his hide. Others targeted Hero, stinging her arms and then her hands as she tried to swat them. Not even Harish was immune. The wasp-bots thickened the air around him, zapping and jolting until he tumbled out of the air with a keening cry. Hero caught him before he hit the ground. Then they were passing through the rectangle of light and leaving the bots behind.

Eventually, they stumbled over the finish line. Fink was panting hard and Harish lay draped over Hero's shoulder. There was no one there to greet them, just a small cluster of drones and Norah waiting patiently in the alley's shadows.

Beyond her, lights and the deep, steady beat of music played in the distance, the silhouette of gyrating arms and bodies thrown against the walls.

Hero slipped off Fink's back, feet as leaden as the guilt sitting on her chest.

'We finished,' Norah said. 'That's something.'

Hero nodded, trying to push the image of all those unconscious racers from her mind.

'We came in last.' Hero lifted Harish from her shoulder and handed the limp bundle of feathers to Norah. 'Now we have no chance of getting into the big race.' *But did it even matter*, Hero thought, *after what she'd just done*?

'Actually, you came third.' Rom's deep voice spoke from somewhere above Fink's head. Fink jumped and snarled, Hero's heart picking up to double-time before she located the almost invisible drone overhead. It dropped out of the sky, coming to hover at head height. 'Most of the field didn't finish.'

Did the drone turn to face her, or was that a trick of the light?

The guilt crawled up the back of Hero's throat. She met Norah's gaze over the drone. The other girl returned it with a tired look of her own. Hero held her breath, waiting for accusation or fear to darken her features, but all she saw were the first stirrings of excitement.

'Norah,' Rom said. 'Touch the drone.'

She did.

A pulse of light flashed from the drone's skin to Norah's bracer. She snatched her hand back with a small gasp, staring at the light as it swarmed over the bio-comp.

'Open your palm,' Rom said.

Their credentials sprang to life over Norah's fingers, the tiny 'pard and 'adder holos casting the alley in a new golden light.

'Congrats, Team Hero. See you at the prelims.'

CHAPTER 7

It was late when they got home, later than it should have been. All the tension that Hero thought she'd left behind in Mina Plaza came back to haunt her. Was the virus she'd planted in the mansion's AI still there? Had Tybalt discovered she'd snuck out? Had her mum?

The elation that had buoyed her after the race had faded somewhere between the lift to the taxi pad and the ride home. It had gone completely by the time Norah stumbled out of the hover, leaving only the nagging sense of time passing.

The tension kept her awake even as the exhaustion rolling off Fink pulled at her bones. It made her stomach twist into knots as she dragged Fink through the gardens, his tail leaving a trail through the flowerbeds and over the lawn.

Some of the tension left Hero's shoulders when she saw the divots left earlier by Fink's paws were gone. A little more of it unwound from her stomach when she saw the mansion windows were dark and realised there was no angry Tybalt waiting for her at the stairs that led to the balcony outside her room.

She held one last sliver of apprehension for the red 'lockdown' message flashing over the balcony doors.

'Abracadabra,' she said.

The doors popped open.

Relief flooded Hero, washing away the nerves and leaving nothing but exhaustion behind as she stepped through the door.

Fink didn't follow, just huffed and collapsed on the balcony, half-asleep before his muzzle touched his paws.

Hero didn't care, with the need for sleep weighing on her, all she cared about was sinking into her mattress and—

A light flicked on.

Tybalt sat in a chair facing the balcony.

Hero froze.

He stared at her, hands folded across his stomach, his expression blank.

She cleared her throat and let her backpack sink to the floor, hoping he didn't see it behind her body. 'I was at Norah's.'

'That's not what her dads said.'

Hero swallowed. 'We didn't stay there.'

'Obviously.' Tybalt's fingers drummed against the back of his clasped hands.

A tension more vicious than when she'd stared down the police stalked up her spine. At least she'd been able to scramble the police's ID scans, but there was no escape from Tybalt's black gaze.

Her thoughts raced but no glib words came to mind.

The silence stretched.

'Did you win?' Tybalt's question broke the tension, but wasn't enough to bring the spit back to her mouth.

'Win what?' she said.

He raised a brow.

Her heart beat a little harder. 'Does Mum know?'

'Know what? That you snuck out of the mansion or that you were street racing?'

Hero's throat worked, but there still wasn't enough moisture in her mouth to swallow. What she needed to know was if her mum knew about Mina Plaza, but she couldn't say that because if Tybalt didn't know, she didn't want to help him find out.

'Any of it,' she finally said.

'Everything. She's not impressed, Hero. You're lucky she's not sending you back to the estate.'

'Oh.' Relief made Hero's shoulders sag. If her mum knew about

Mina Plaza, *not impressed* wouldn't begin to cover her reaction, and sending her back into exile would be the least of it. Try throwing her in a padded cell and poking her with hypo-sticks.

Hero picked up the bag and dragged it across the room, dumping it by the bed.

'How did you get out, Hero?' It was more of a command than a question and Hero answered without thinking.

'Abracadabra.' She mumbled as the exhaustion pulled her eyes closed and she flopped back on the bed.

'What?'

'Abracadabra,' she said again, this time more loudly.

Distantly, she heard the balcony doors open.

Sleep was pulling her under, filling her eyelids with drones, companions and the steady flash of police lights. She barely felt Tybalt take off her boots or swing her legs onto the mattress and only noticed the blanket settling over her legs as an absence of the cold.

'Hero?'

'Hmm?'

'You're grounded.'

'Okay,' she said again, and let sleep pull her all the way under.

DO YOU WANT MORE HERO?

I love keeping in touch with my readers, it's the second-best thing about being a writer (writing being the first best). Every fortnight (or thereabouts), I send out a newsletter with details about upcoming offers, new releases and extra special projects.

If you sign up for the mailing you'll receive exclusive behind-the-scenes extras, such as:

- free short stories
- deleted and alternate scenes from The Hero Rebellion
- previews of my upcoming books
- pancakes
- quizes
- and much, much more!

Sign up here

news.belindacrawford.com/newsletter

ACKNOWLEDGMENTS

Race may be a fraction of the length of *Hero*, but there was no shortage of people who have helped me get it into your hands.

As always, thanks go to my editor, Brendan Carney, who worked his usual magic, and to my beta readers, Tracy M Joyce and Jennifer Richardson. A second "thank you" goes to Jennifer, proofreader extraordinaire, for finding all of those niggling spelling errors that both Brendan and I missed.

These wonderful people were instrumental in whipping Race into shape, both grammatically and structurally, and without whom *The Hero Rebellion* wouldn't be the same.

ABOUT THE AUTHOR

Physics makes Belinda's brain hurt, while quadratics cause her eyes to cross and any mention of probability equations will have her running for the door. Nonetheless, she loves watching documentaries about the natural world, biology, space, history and technology.

She's also a sucker for a fast horse, a faster computer and superhero movies. When she's not doing the horse, computer or superhero thing, Belinda writes science fiction (emphasis on the fiction), where she loves to write about butt-kicking girls who blow stuff up.

You can keep in touch with Belinda, or just pick her brains about sci-fi via her website, Facebook or by sending her an email (she loves email).

www.belindacrawford.com
belinda@belindacrawford.com

Have news delivered straight to your inbox
via her mailing list. Sign up at:
news.belindacrawford.com/newsletter